This book belongs to

....

No. 1

Published in 2010
by Igloo Books Ltd
Cottage Farm
Sywell
NN6 OBJ
www.igloo-books.com

Original story by Igloo Books Ltd.
© Hallmark Cards PLC
Forever Friends is a trademark of Hallmark Cards PLC
www.foreverfriends.com

B044 0410
10 9 8 7 6 5 4 3
ISBN: 9781848529519

Printed and manufactured in China

Daddy & Me

igloo

My daddy is very special and
I love him very much.

Every day, Daddy plays games with me.

"I'm sailing a boat."

When we go to the park, Daddy
helps me fly my aeroplane...

... and teaches me to
play ball games.

I like it when he watches me
ride my skateboard.

"Look how fast I can go."

My daddy teaches me
how to mend things...

... and he lets me
play computer games
with my friends.

I like it when Daddy watches me
bounce on my trampoline.

"Look how high I can jump."

When we play outside, Daddy
helps me search for bugs...

... and he pushes me
in my toy car.

Daddy shows me how to plant seeds.

"They will grow in to big plants."

When we go to the river, Daddy shows me how to sail my boat...

... and teaches me how to catch the biggest fish!

When we go to the beach, Daddy
teaches me how to surf.

"Look at the big waves."

I like it when my daddy
plays dress-up with me...

... and when he gives me crayons
so I can draw pictures.

I like it when he helps me ride my toy train.

"Choo-choo."

When it snows, my daddy
teaches me to snowboard...

... and he pulls me on the sledge.

I like it when Daddy helps me build a snowman.

"My snowman has a carrot for a nose."

At the end of each day,
Daddy wraps me up
after my bath...

... and he gives me
my cuddly toy before
tucking me into bed.

To show my daddy how much I love him,
I'm going to wash his car.

I'm going to help tidy up...

... and make yummy cakes.

I'll make him a nice breakfast.

And I'll give him a special card.

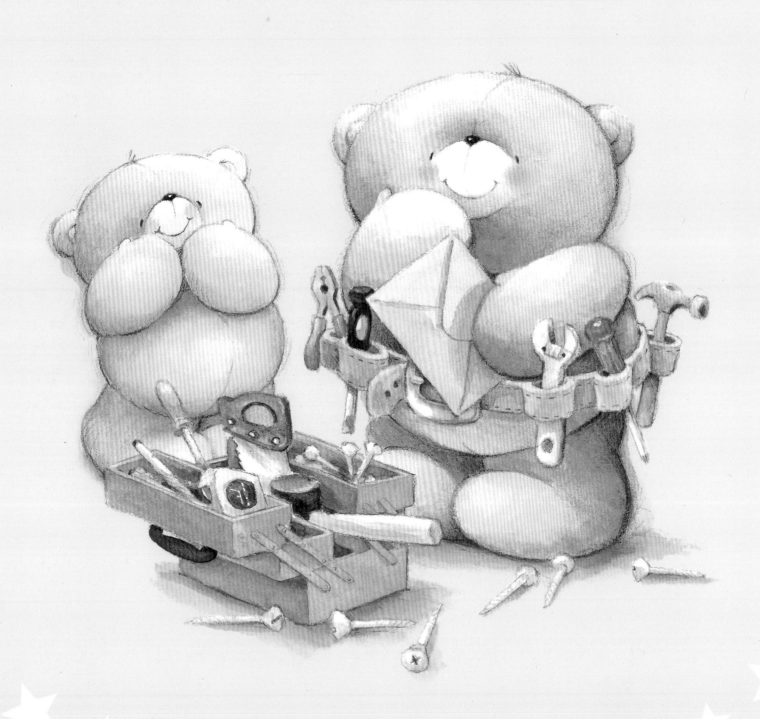

My daddy is the best daddy
in the whole world!

I love you, Daddy!